THE WIND BENEATH MY WINGS

JOHN HUTCHINSON CONCORDE PILOT

SUSAN OTTAWAY

LUME BOOKS

LUME BOOKS

This edition published in 2021 by Lume Books
30 Great Guildford Street,
Borough, SE1 0HS

Copyright © Susan Ottaway 2011

The right of Susan Ottaway to be identified as the author of this work has been asserted by them in accordance with the Copyright, Design and Patents Act, 1988.

All rights reserved. No part of this publication may be reproduced, stored in a retrieval system, or transmitted in photocopying, recording or otherwise, without the prior permission of the copyright owner.

ISBN 978-1-83901-432-1

Typeset using Atomik ePublisher from Easypress Technologies

www.lumebooks.co.uk

For Nick

KC's Emporium of Wet Dreams
By

Also by Katrina Chanice

KC's Emporium of Wet Dreams
Melanin Midas Empire

Katrina Chanice

Stay Connected

SnapChat: @bookbaddiekc

Copyright 2024 Katrina Chanice
All rights reserved
The characters and events portrayed in this book are fictitious. Any similarity to real persons, living or dead, is coincidental and not intended by the author.
No part of this book may be reproduced, stored in a retrieval system, or transmitted in any form or by any means, electronic, mechanical, photocopying, recording, or otherwise, without express wrote permission of the publisher.

Table of Contents

1. Three's A Crowd (More by Silk)
2. Face of Olay (Power by Kevin Gates)
3. Video Vixen (Nasty by Joshua Showtime Williams)
4. The MisEducation of Sex (Jupiter Love by Trey Songz)
5. I Am A Good Girl (Good For You by Selena Gomez ft. A$AP Rocky)
6. Unapologetically Wicked (Lick by Joi)
7. Shrimp N' Grits (Surprise by Chole Bailey)
8. ShowKaze (Blow Your Back Out by Tha Joker)

Writing has its ups and downs like so many other things in life. For me it started as therapeutic and yet it became something totally different. Something that I could simply play around with while learning a slew of new skills that I can contribute to other projects in my life such as my kids' YouTube show. The thought of remaining as an anonymous writer did cross my mind since I wanted to keep my home life completely separate from my author life but in the end it's all one life. I would be doing myself a disservice to not give it all of me every single time. I've simply taken the time to explore the pleasurable side of what God created as a reward for being married and fruitful. It's an expression of love....one of many obviously and understanding what works for you and your spouse is the most important things to do first before attempting to dive into waters you're not used to. I only hope to add a little spice to your life through the art of literature. I'm happy with my man (my favorite fan) y'all. Not all couples want monogamy and not all couples want a polyamorous lifestyle. I'm an equal opportunity writer...meaning I write about ALL lifestyles. My writing is a reflection of life & art.

This short story was simple, written within maybe thirty minutes with a few officers of the law in mind. I had to stay true and use the location that inspired the writing. After a quick chat with a sweet little lady sharing with me how her open marriage had landed her behind bars, a light bulb went off. My absolute favorite story within this collection as it was the first that went on to inspire the others.

Three's A Crowd

"Can we embrace each other...while the moon gives light...can we make a pact to stay together forever...forever together" – More by Silk

Not in a million years did I think that I'd be sitting beside Shaun with a Cuban cigar in one hand and a Tom Collins in the other while watching my wife plant her pretty thick ass on the face of a Victoria Secret's model that Shaun had been married to for the last sixteen years. I've been working under this man as a sergeant for well over five years. From my understanding, he was a man that fully loved his wife and never once stepped out. The same can be said for Gabriella. Their marriage of love and commitment was something me and my wife adored and fully respected. I'm not sure how we ended up in the penthouse suite of the Hilton with Usher's *'Can You Handle It'* playing softly in the background.

We shared an anniversary of October 10th and for the last three or four years, we've shared anniversary dates and trips. It's been the highlight of my love's life. The Sunday school teacher of our church and a stay-at-home mom of our two boys that's married to a newly promoted lieutenant of Rankin County Jail. We lived a simple life and until now we assumed the sheriff and his wife did as well.

Gabriella's hands gripped my wife's voluptuous hips, digging her fingertips in as my wife moaned swirling her body in a circular motion as if she was trying to win a hoola hoop competition. Just on the verge of busting through my charcoal grey slacks when Shaun stood up walking towards the bed. I closed my eyes and shook my heal. It's quite possible that God wasn't hearing a damn thing that I was saying. I didn't want to kill this man for touching my wife.

The memory of Anastasia waltzing out of the bathroom, arms locked in with Gabriella as they giggled over what I assumed was something about the kids or some reality show that they both enjoyed, quickly flashed before my eyes. An anniversary dinner after enjoying a Morgan Wallen concert at Black Axes is all that this night was supposed to consist of. When Anastasia sat down beside me, she placed her balled up fist inside of my hand passing me her balled up slightly moisten black silk underwear. Her sweetness was a scent that I could detect a mile away. My wife was in heat. Something I knew all too well when she's had a few too many daiquiris. I'm not sure how we ended up in the penthouse suite of the Hilton with the sheriff plowing his wife while planting kisses on my wife's ass as she continued to swirl her thick ass on his wife's face. I watched with an odd sense of satisfaction. It was intriguing to see exactly how this night would end.

Anastasia locked eyes with me, mouthing the words, *'I love you'* while I downed the rest of my drink. She never lost rhythm as the song changed to *'So Anxious'* by Ginuwine. I suppose the plan was to disrupt her flow as much as possible. Remind her that this was a one-time thing. It wasn't happening again. Just as I stood up, Shaun was dropping to his knees going on to devour his pretty little wife. I knew that I didn't want a taste and yet I was licking my lips with an intense ache to plant kiss along his wife's ample little ass just as he had done mine. The thought quickly disappeared as I stood firmly on the bed with my rod entering my wife's perfect little mouth.

Anastasia had changed so much since she met Gabriella, claiming to have found herself after having the boys. I fully enjoyed the new woman that had emerged from within my wife. It was my assumption that Gabriella was simply a good friend and that was something I knew my wife needed, however Anastasia's never ridden my face before. From the way Gabriella seemed so content with slurping my wife until the break of dawn suggested that this had to have happened a few times already. Before tonight I wasn't allowed to even touch her hair but, in this moment, Anastasia had taken my hands, placing them on the back of her head where I grabbed a fistful of her beautifully highlighted silk pressed hair and fucked my wife's prefect little mouth until I exploded in the back of her throat. She looked at me with a smile while wiping a drop of cum from the corner of her mouth.

I'm not sure how we ended up in the penthouse suite of the Hilton with Shaun slow stroking Anastasia while massaging her swollen clit as I hammered down Gabriella's tight walls from the back only to become more aroused from the two beautiful goddesses tongue each other down. Not in a million years did I think that I'd be planting kisses on the sheriff's wife's ass causing her to turn around and swallow up my whole dick while Shaun had my wife against the wall, legs on his shoulders eating her up like a crazed red nose pit. Maybe a few more times wouldn't be so bad.....

For Bishop Walls & Queen Mother (Lester & Donna)

Contrary to popular belief writing erotic stories makes me blush so hard. Even though I joke about being Beyonce of Mississippi, I constantly find myself in the same zone as she was when recording the song *'Partition'* because MY GOD girly what in the *'Church Girl'* is going on here?!

As I stated in the previous note to my oh so lovable readers, I at one point wanted to be an anonymous writer. My home life consisted of being a stay at home, a Sunday school teacher, and a nursing student having just had my third child. Once I dropped a few bags.... clearly I was wearing myself thin....I focused only on being a stay at home mom and getting closer to God. I didn't at all want my kids, their friends and certainly not my grandma..... although it was Meme(Linda) that stated *'It's a book about life'* I couldn't argue with the statement....all of my books are truly just books about life...so here I am....Mrs. Smut & Starbucks!

This story, as many actually are, is simply a remixed moment in time that I had with BestFriend(Showout). The more I popped up.... literally everywhere(home, job, favorite hangout spot)... the more he urged me to stop popping up and at least call first. He knows how much I adore his reactions to my spontaneity and unpredictable behavior. I will indeed pop up on all of my family as my true friend know they are my adopted family(on my non ghost days). BestFriend is not special in this sense, he's just the only one that tells me not to do it while blushing something terrible causing me to do it more.

I'm so thankful to his brother from another mother(the BuzzLight Year to his Woody) for not ever having an issue with my pop ups and indulging my crazy shenanigans while teasing my poor BestFriend in good faith the way that brothers naturally do with one another.

Face of Olay

"That lil' pussy got some power in it. That lil' pussy got some power in it. Super soaker, need a towel for it. Drippin' on me like a showerhead" –
Power by Kevin Gates

The solemn look on his face told me everything that I needed to know. His anger was extremely clear to the entire neighborhood of FernValley as he stood in the doorway attempting to deny my entrance into the house that he shared with his brother. Too many devious thoughts rushed through my mind, clouding my judgement, causing me to see this man as irresistible while wondering why he'd step out waring only his gym shorts and Nike slides. My eyes drifted to his V-Line and subsequently to my harden friend.

My lady moistened in response, dripping with full desire for this one man that was refusing my entrance into the house that I once called a whorehouse. If only for a few minutes I hoped he'd break the rules just for me. He missed me, despite his effort at turning me away, his body had responded in the same exact way that mine had. We missed each other. Eventually he noticed how none of his anger filled goodbye speech meant anything to me as I stepped closer, gently stroking his V-Line while asking coyly, "A kiss before I go?"

The corner of his lips jerked. I knew what the answer would be. Another attempt at trying to hide his true feelings as he sighed and wrapped his arms around my waist, pulling me closer into his embrace and whispered, "Last time."

A sense of triumph came over me as he stepped backwards into the house. Each stop filled with kisses of ecstasy guiding are down the hallway to his bedroom. Not a second longer and I had already ripped out of every piece of article of clothing that I had on. He smirked, fully entertained at the scene displayed before him. His truest intentions now shining clear as ever as he walked up to me passionately kissing me into his bed of love. Mischievous and playful is what I adored about the man and with me he allowed his naughty side to take over. He peeled out of his gym shorts and stood up completely naked, in all of his magnificent glory.

My lady purred as I watched him slowly stroking his Mandingo warrior. He chuckled and stated, "You can't keep popping up like this."

I nodded eagerly without saying a word, knowing that in a matter of days, I'd be popping up again for another 'last time.' As soon as he placed his index and middle finger within me, his thumb and two fingers massaged my clit forcing me to bite down on my bottom lip. A well known addiction. My obsession with this man was no secret to the neighbors and especially not his brother from the many times that I've been forced to be a bit quieter because his brother has to get up extremely early in the morning. The obvious that seems to escape my mind from the touch of his hands on my body.

Suddenly he had pulled me to the edge of the bed and slowly glided his pulsating Mandingo warrior inside of me until every inch of his thickness filled me up, stretching me completely out, sending electrifying thrills of pleasure coursing through my body. Uncontrollable shivers from the only man that knew how to properly please me. That knew at any given moment, I'd be ringing his doorbell begging for more of his sweet loving. Slow and steady were his strokes. He was simply warming up. Soon the true beast would emerge. I placed my hands around the back of his head bringing his face closer to mine. Light pecks quickly turned into gentle nibbles on his bottom lip trailing to his earlobe and down his neck onto his chest.

Within his moans, he whispered, "Is this what you wanted baby?"
Barely able to respond, I simply stutter, "Y y y y yesssss."
A low growl escaped from his lips as his strokes sped up. Just as we kissed once more, he pulls out and switches up to what he has claimed

has his favorite position. In reality it was mine and he had yet to see all of the many different ways I wanted to express my love to him in this armless dining room chair. Of course, he wasn't ready for the cowgirl workout I had concocted in my mind as he waited anxiously for me to straddle him in a position, he had learned how to take control in.

Confusion rested on his face as I turned around and mounted my Mandingo warrior in reverse cowgirl. With my legs spread wide and my hands planted firmly on his thighs, I bounced for the gold as well as his soul. I knew I already had his heart. The tingling sensation from the way his hand slapped my ass cheek while his other hand palmed my breasts resulted in me sitting up straight, arching my back to feel his Mandingo warrior effortlessly rearrange my insides. It wasn't long before he was pushing my thick thighs together and my arch become a wave of orgasmic pleasure. Without missing a beat, I turned my head to the left and spoke softly, "You like this?"

In a low and raspy voice, he replied, "Yes baby."

As soon as I was about to twerk him into submission, he grabbed both of my wrists, pulling my arms behind me as he stood up unlocking a new position for us to reminisce on later. The beast had fully emerged. I was done for. Vigorously, he rammed his Mandingo warrior swelling up my walls until I moaned out loudly probably fully disturbing the entire neighborhood and especially his brother's peaceful slumber. The louder I moaned, the harder he rammed as if he wanted to spilt me in half. A single tear formed and slid down my cheek while my mouth hung open wide, and my eyes rolled to the back of my head.

A pleasure I would gladly offer to pay for. If he wanted to rip both arms off, I would happily oblige. Within an instant, he had let go of my arms and started digging his fingertips into my hips. Harder and faster, he went with beads of sweat dripping on to the small of my back. I placed my hands on the floor for a bit of support when he stopped his strokes and instantly my legs went limp. There my harden Mandingo friend bobbed up and down so beautifully in his hand as he stroked once more with a smirk. While placing my hands on the back of his thighs, he begins to stroke my throat as hums of pure joy escaped from within me.

The back of his hand gently brushed against my cheek as he said, "Damn, you're beautiful." Just as pulled out of my throat, he had blasted his load all over my face, using his Mandingo warrior to rub it around my cheeks and into my mouth as I thought to myself, *'Damn, I love this man!'*

For John & Makayla

It's the Age of Technology. Communication has been simplified to nothing more than a few emojis between family, friends, and lovers. Family reunions replaced with group chats. Old photo albums now a collection of Google photos shared constantly on social media. The saddest part is how social media interactions....a like, a command, a follow, a share...had been deemed as cheating.

Social media is where most of my readers reside and I have most certainly interacted with them while showcasing my personality and draw attention to my page which has my works of art displayed. A social media portfolio if you will. While being in a relationship my man would have to be more than understanding that nothing that I do on the internet should be seen as vanity or a cry for attention. Baby I'm WORKING.....you gone match my energy or what???

The idea behind this next short came from......drumroll please.....BESTFRIEND! Two years ago, his brother Evan and the beautiful Nikita were joined together in holy matrimony in Sweet Home Alabama. BestFriend was gone for maybe a week or so and I thought myself, *'If this was my man then I'd send him a little naughty video.'* Nothing too too naughty.....a tease if you will. It's a must to keep your man craving you at all times even when you're miles apart. The beauty of technology!

Video Vixen

"I love the way you taste. Pull my hair and say my name. I'll grip you tight you can't escape" – Nasty by Joshua Showtime Williams

I'm sure it was disappointing to see the pole down, but it would've only been wicked temptation and I sir am not a temptress. A tease, however, a tease I most certainly am. So yes, I unscrewed the pole just before you arrived. You came over to handle business and I want you to stay focused. Stay the course. The pole would've been a distraction. Filling your mind with naughty thoughts that you did not need. I sir am your friend. Always steering you clear of even your own poor decisions. Yet, you fault me! You say that I have enabled you to go against your better judgement while yearning to partake with me once more. Eventually you will.

Your phone dinged back to back. Notification after notification. All coming from me and now you're worried for no reason and yet it was you that opened the message. It was you that watched the video.....over and over again.....and again and again.....and then once more for the road. A quick look while at work....how would anybody ever know. Another on the road and I suppose one last look before bed, maybe now you'll dream of this scene tonight instead. I wasn't at all aware of your scheduled *'me time'* and yet....you fault me!

It was you that agreed to work late. It was you and the many work trips. Boredom set in when I suddenly found myself adjusting the angle of the camera just right for this one bedroom scene. Learning the pole hasn't been easy and I only trust your feedback on the results.....

Silence.....

Crickets.....

I wanted an answer I suppose. Nothing else worked. The attachment of me in the hot tub. The attachment of me in the shower. The attachment of the solo twerkathon. The attachment of my ass clapping effortlessly...... no feedback from you.

So in position I go. Parting my lips and dramatically dipping in and out of my ocean. If you were here, no dramatics would be needed but to be a witness unto my own naughtiness requires a bit of theatrics....especially for myself. Simple encouragement and yet you fault me! I missed you and I knew you'd love watching me making figure eights on my throbbing clit. Yes, you'd absolutely go wild hearing me moan your name as I palm my breasts, fingers swirling with a mind of its own. You'd stare with your mouth open as I suck my sweet juices off my middle finger.

You'd moan while instructing me to do something.....anything as long as it seemed as if we were in the same room. In that same moment.....together. Bodies entwined with no deadline for relief. And yet you fault me....for your wicked enjoyment.

You should've been here..... instead I was all alone with nothing but dirty thoughts of you.

I suppose it is indeed my fault as you believe I want to use you to recreate scenes rather than use you to invent new scenes. Let's practice both and see what we come up with. A temptress. You're right. It is my fault. I'll have the pole up next time.

All props will remain on set.....

For Evan & Nikita

As odd as this little note may be, here we are! While diving into writing and publishing naturally I came across a few haters. My love for writing has produced works of art that I consider my babies. In the same sense that many will rip you a new one for dismissing their parenthood to their furbabies, I was ready to taser a few haters in their vaginas/groins about my babies (kids, books, & man).

Naturally haters are simply fans and I do love all of my fans. A fan does not have to be a reader but most likely they are and I love you even more for being fans of my art rather than fans of drama or an image but something that I've actually worked at creating. MUAH!!!!

The MisEducation of Sex

"Don't you be afraid to...Let me elevate you...Welcome you to super, duper, Jupiter love." – Jupiter Love by Trey Songz

A class full of misfits laughing about being the man in these streets. What exactly required them to state such a claim? I had signed up for the educational class per my counselor's request. Nothing here that I needed to learn. This was now court mandated. Just here for the certificate and I'll never be seen here again. Soon the door flung open and in walked a beautiful cinnamon brown beauty that was the best image to look at when learning master skills for the master bedroom.

Wearing black bellbottoms that hugged her ample bottom just right. The white turtleneck and black spenders gave her more of a schoolgirl look instead of the image of a teacher which I went from assuming to hoping that she was. Luck was on my side as she sat down behind the desk not saying a word with her eyes locked in on the class of maybe 10 guys. The school like chatter we had going amongst ourselves, quickly died down into a complete silence. She continued to sit quietly. Her chin comfortably settled onto her hands where her fingers were entwined.

If she was bored, then she hid it extremely well. She seemed content but her patience granted her the stage she knew was already hers. Eventually she stood up and came around to the front of the desk to say, "Let's not have to be here any longer than we have to be. This class is only optional. It's not something that you have to do and by all means you're more than welcome to leave right now." She paused with her hand held out towards the door, giving us time to make the decision to leave. Maybe I was the only one with a court mandated order to come to class. The thought to leave crossed mind and yet I wondered what was she about to teach as she continued, "Let's hope that the ones staying are actually willing to learn."

As soon as she stood up, she'd gathered up the packets that sat at the end of her desk and passed them out to each guy sitting at a desk thinking the same exact thing that I was. We all did the same exact thing. All of us. There wasn't one original cat in the bunch. Attempting to give her a look while licking our lips that we knew pulled every other girl no problem. She must've been a lesbian. Makes sense. No way a woman as beautiful as her was going to teach a class like this to a bunch of men while maintaining her composure. She's definitely a lesbian. I shrugged and ignored her. No need in flirting with a brick wall.

My lack of interaction caused her to call me out for each and every example. Granted they were all great examples. The class learned with ease. Affection. Being attentive. After-Care..... the ABC's for the pleasurable art of intercourse. As a woman she taught us the beauty in understanding not only your body but your partner's body as well. No point in pleasing the body when the mind is obviously lost. No mind was more lost than mine as I replayed a recent conversation in my mind while accepting my place as a *'findom'* and already knowing the perfect *'finsub'* living just a couple of states over.

The class inquired about the teacher's sexual personality, she smiled and replied, "I like big rigs."

So, it was obvious that she liked truck drivers until she taught us about rigging which I had completely confused with edging. A 2-hour long class that I have to take for the next 6 weeks and I had already failed the pop quiz that was about my damn self! It's about the motion in the ocean and not the size of the boat. Something we'd been led to believe the complete opposite. Miss lady had solutions and strategies that broaden our horizons. The homework was to incorporate the new karma sutra positions into the bedroom. We'd learned about the ones best suited for mutual stimulation with our partners.

The last to gather my notes and actually head out the door. The coolest lady I had ever met and maybe she had a friend that wasn't so into women like her. A single man taking a court mandated sex class. *'How was I supposed to effectively do my homework,'* I thought to myself. My hope that going out for drinks wouldn't fall on deaf ears. I had learned a lot and wanted to learn so much more. From the court mandated class to drinks at Last Call and back to my place in downtown Jackson, Mississippi. She agreed to a night of blissful insanity while practicing positions and sexual healing for the brokenhearted that I refused to share with anybody else.

She walked around full of confidence, playing in her long honey blonde curls while wearing only a small black spaghetti strap tank top as she says, "Every man in my class is a married man except you. You're court mandated."

With my back leaning against the headboard, I smiled wide while saying, "Signed off by General Mills."

She chuckled as she climbed back into the bed, her hands already gently massaging my semi erect rod. Using each finger to juggle my dick and balls within her grasp. She catches me completely off guard as she says, "So my father sent you?"

My eyes flew open, and my mouth followed. Stuck in a state of shock. The only movement my body could register from her words. The rest of my body only understood the warmth of her mouth as her pretty tight lips wrapped around my shaft sliding up and down. Her tongue swirling around the tip like an ice cream cone that she was enjoying licking more and more. The only control I had was holding back this nut but if I continued to enjoy this sorcery, I'd be blasting all in her honey golden curls.

A mind reader of some sorts. She stopped within seconds of my release as she giggled. I pleaded with her to continue and all she did was giggle more as I stroked and blasted off on myself. The realization of the connection between us became more apparent but quickly dismissed when she started rubbing her hands over her body, moaning and enjoying herself. I didn't say a word. Wasn't sure what needed to be said but I was rock hard all over again and this time I was making her my little toaster strudel.

Slow and steady. I didn't want her to stop anything that she was doing to herself. My only goal was to increase her pleasure. Her fingers rubbed her clit matching the speed of my strokes. As my speed increased, her massaging swirls turned into rapid circles. Her juices flowed harder causing my knees to buckle feeling the grips of her walls tighten around my shaft. Her fingers still making mini hurricanes, drawing me near. Just as I had vowed to myself, I blasted off on her beautiful frame. She continued to massage her clit and moan to the feel of my warm nut cooling on her stomach.

A man that now understood after-care, I wondered about my next steps. That's when I remembered, miss lady had some explaining to do about General Mills being her father. I went into the bathroom and started up the jetted roman tub, still had so much to learn from this sexual goddess.

For Andre 'DJ MoneyHungry' Carter

Considering the recent events in my life.....such a cruel summer....I've decided to take a walk on the wild side with this one.....hoping to create a little humor for a good girl gone bad. It was.....as always....a random moment with BestFriend in OUR OFFICE that led to him screaming out, *'You're a bad girl!'* Now granted I had just put him in a headlock.....playfully obviously and I've been deemed *'a bad girl'* in his eyes ever since. Can't seem to get right for nothing.

Ironically, I was not at all happy with the statement and slightly offended. I considered myself to be a damn good girl!!!! And then....well writing has been truly an amazing journey and we're just going to accept it for what it is. He's hardly ever wrong and I've certainly been proving him right since he screamed it out. I think it's something rather magical in being able to be the sweetest and nastiest person for your spouse. Making sure that person feels safe in every single way, especially in their most vulnerable state.

A guy was waiting for his girl to get out of jail and she seemed to be such a nice girl. Innocent and sweet and blah blah blah but regardless of what she looked like to others....to HER MAN she was indeed innocent and sweet and blah blah blah which is exactly how he should see her and vice versa.

Then again......

We can take this imagination train for a ride....

I Am A Good Girl

"I just wanna look good for you, good for you, oh-oh. Baby, let me be good to you, good to you, oh-oh. Let me show you how proud I am to be yours." – Good For You by Selena Gomez ft A$AP Rocky

As soon as I made it to the end of the parking lot, there he stood across the street at the gas station locking eyes on me with his arms folded because I had once again ignored his instructions when it came to handling any of my affairs like I had promised him I would well over six months ago. As soon as I made it to him, he smiled while throwing his arms around swinging my entire body into a circle as he said, "Baby I missed you!"

It was extremely comforting to hear the words and to witness the display of concern for my wellbeing, but we had rather more important pressing matters and I needed desperately to get as far away from the scene as possible. He sensed how alert I was and understood my desire to leave the place that had housed me for the last thirty days on what I screamed out were bogus charges. Anything to get me released. Not quick enough and this cute little Honda Civic wasn't going fast enough.

A sigh of relief escaped my lips, and I felt safer to breathe. My mind racing a million miles per hour while this guy continuously expressed how much he missed me and how much he loved me. Words that seeped in one ear and spilled out of the other. Nothing he said did I actually register and when we pulled up to the house, I hoped like hell it would be a quick minute or two. Of course, I wasn't ready for the reunion and just my luck he comes around to the passenger side and opens my door. Knowing that I can't refuse the next few moments of pure agony, I swallow my pride and face the consequences of my actions.

Just as I thought, his parents are elated. Praises of my safe return while I still felt trapped and stuck in a hell that I had seemingly created for myself. His dad went outside with the grands while his mom went back to entertaining all of the guests that she'd invited to warmly welcome me back home. The mission was successful since the only thing truly needed was to cancel a transaction and although we were in the clear, my face refused to give a genuine smile. Unable to fake the funk any longer and I say, "Baby, I really need to talk to you in the back of the house."

Without any hesitation, he escorts me to the first bedroom door in the house which is directly across from the guest bathroom. Thinking if I should slip into the bathroom first or just get it over with in the bedroom. I wasn't sure how this should go but maybe enticing a little sex might help this to go over a little more easily than slipping into the bathroom as if I'm actually guilty because I'm not. I'm totally innocent.

His smile came from the belief that I was about to fuck his brains out in his old childhood bedroom and maybe I was however my understanding was clear as I said, "I need a favor."

He knew I would as I no longer had a car, job, or place to live and luck simply wasn't on my side with him being at the gas station upon my release and him bringing me to the family house to have a safe place to stay. The sweetest guy I know and the only one I trusted with my truth of deceit. He held me close while laying his head within my bosom as he said, "Anything you need baby."

I sighed and without saying another word, I grabbed his hand slipping it into my pants, allowing his fingers to naturally begin to caress my pearl. Quickly becoming aroused, I needed to stay on task as I spoke softly, "Further."

Instantly, he went faster while ripping my breasts out of the top of my shirt, suckling on my erect nipples. My moans grew when he whispered, "I love you."

With a nod, I stayed on task as I said slightly above a whisper, "Further baby."

He groaned denying my request only to go even faster. I held on to his head for dear life and he enjoyed the moment until he finally went further and stopped all production as he boldly said, "What the fuck?!"

It was fun while it lasted. When his hand emerged from my overly saturated and anxiously throbbing fun box, in his hand was a mini makeshift dildo. He looked at me with utter shock on his face waiting for me to explain myself. I didn't. The understanding was clear the moment he pulled the contraband out of my fun box. He knew I had been arrested on conspiracy charges and even took the time to clear my name in that. I absolutely didn't know a thing about any armed robberies and stolen jewelry. The charges were outrageous even down to the drugs. Some I had never even heard of before my little stint in lock up. It took everything in me not to run away but I trusted him, and I hoped he'd hear me out despite the fact that the words never formed. The contents within the heavily wrapped plastic wrap were obvious as we had been looking for this particular flash drive for years. The information it contained could bring down too many of this world's wealthiest families. From the oil tycoons of the Al Nayhan family to the wealthy Willy Wonka of our universe, the Mars family. The same family that almost cut ties with us for good only a few short months before I was arrested.

Speechless was the word. The way his eyes went from his hand to my eyes and back to his hand said everything that he couldn't manage to say. I could've been like Chicken Little and had it just fell from the sky and the safest place to hide it was buried deep within me. I could've thrown my hands up, giving up while saying it just appeared snuggled behind my g-spot. The truth was I was praying the fucking thing still worked. It was never my intention to use my fun box as my very own pandora's box but as they say, *'desperate times call for desperate measures.'* After the flashing blue lights caught my attention and I finally stopped, my half eaten sandwich sitting in the plastic wrap that I had previously wrapped as a snack on the road was now flashing like a neon sign.

The moment the officer walked away from the window; I knew I was going to jail. All of my constituents had faced the fire except me. How lovely to finally find the long lost flash drive just to get arrested on the day I find it. A quick wrap session and up my vagina it went. It was exhilarating for the first ninety days and then paranoia grew, and I knew it was more than time to get on down. Here I stood before the one person that had my back screaming to the world that I was innocent of EVERYTHING was holding the very flash drive that I had been accused of having for all of these years. Suddenly, he had tossed the flash drive to the side of the bed, pulling me onto him as he says with a smile, "You're a bad girl!"

Nothing about this moment was supposed to end like this. Not with me nibbling on his neck while bouncing happily on my favorite criminal mastermind. The Clyde to my Bonnie. With a quick tap, I leaned up and he was guiding me towards his face. A ride I wasn't at all ready for as his thick tongue slightly stiffened while swirling around inside of my fun box. I scratched at the headboard attempting not to scream out from the uncommon sorcery that was taking place. Tipping over like the cash cow that I was believing this warranted a small conversation at the least, it didn't. He was on me like white on rice, continuing to slurp me up as I tried my best to run away.

While holding my body, he continues to boost my head up as he says, "You feel so good."

He's filled me up so many times before as I've always tried to be a good girl. So gentle and sweet. Never once stepping into the dark side and being too rough. I've always been his future wife and it's well known that a man can't slut out his wife. That's what the whores are for! Well, my future husband accidentally on purpose slutted me out for being a bad girl. The way that man slightly squeezed my neck spitting into my mouth while wrecking my ovaries had me squirting hard all over his childhood bed.

For Tutu (Lester Reuben Walls)

Often times I've stated that I live vicariously through others as they freely share with me their sexual explorations. Many of the stories are told by different individuals that sound so similar to books and movies that I've seen, so I make my own little versions. Originally, I wanted this collection of short erotic stories to be titled *'Sexcapades: Wild Fantasies'* which at the time was highly appropriate since I had asked several men and women about their sexual fantasies and just like a game of Family Feud...the #1 answer was a threesome and *'The Masquerade Ball'* was invented.

Instead of moving forward with *'Sexcapades: Wild Fantasies'* I combined my first collection of short stories and my first novel *'Secrets of my Heart's Desire'* together and created *'Melanin Midas Empire: A Dark Royal Romance.'* A statement from Stephen King, that I truly take to heart which is a writer's work is never truly complete and remakes can be made as many times as they prefer which is the reason this little short is a special thank you to ALL of the bikers in the world....the bad boys on 2 wheels. They definitely hold a special place in my heart, mind, and soul. I adore them for being unapologetically them and always standing on business!

Unapologetically Wicked

"I lose all control. When you grab a hold. And you do your trick. I love it when you lick" – Lick by Joi

'I'M SURE OF IT.'
'They think I'm high.'
'Scared, shy, and high.'

These were the thoughts running through my mind as I stood off to the side of the dance floor watching a few bust some familiar moves. I could've joined in but I needed to watch the door. He'd be here at any moment. I've missed him every single time that he's posted an event which is why I came early like I was a part of the set up crew. I just needed to see if he's real or does he only exist on the internet. Too many bets going against me saying that my man is just fucking AI. They were crushing my hopes before they even got started good stating it's just been awhile since I've had a man and that he's probably using filters but that's only if he's a real person. Today, I was going to prove it all wrong.

And prove it wrong I did. Or maybe I was wrong.....

In an instance, I was swept up in a rather sticky situation. It was dark. My hands were bound above my head to a hook with a rope of some sort. Very secured. They must've had practiced hog tying on the daily. No surprise that my feet were bound as well spread nicely apart while the entire bedframe felt elevated. Whispers and chuckles surrounded me and the coolness of an ice cube slid across my already erect nipple followed up by the warmth of a rather thick tongue. Slowly I inhaled, unable to remove the blindfold that kept my punisher hidden. It was stated as the restraints were placed, "This is the only way to tame your wild ass. You need to learn boundaries."

A different voice followed behind saying, "Why must you be so damn hardheaded?!"

While suppressing a laugh, I nodded with understanding as I was already aroused from being in their presence. I happily indulged in the festivities with each smiling face as they all knew exactly who I was and had planned months in advance on how it would be best to put me in my place. The beginning of my sexual intervention and I was already enjoying it entirely too much. The agony slowly heated my honey pot. The fingertips of several different hands brushed against my body. Different areas all set ablaze at the same time. Both erect nipples being suckled by two different mouths. I continued to slowly inhale. The exhale was staggered. As fingers massaged my throbbing clit, another hand took the time to slowly submerge within my honey pot as many fingers as he could. Too many hands to count. Too many sensations. Still, I slowly inhaled, fully enjoying the company of my punishers.

A deep familiar voice whispered in my ear, "Be quiet."

Confusion set on my face that could only be read by my frowned eyebrows underneath the blindfold. The confusion quickly dispersed from the way my honey pot fit perfectly in the mouth of one of my punishers while the deep familiar voice nibbled on my earlobe, planting kisses until helping me to cheat by keeping me quiet with his tongue down my throat. Hands continued to palm my breasts, massaging and lightly pinching my nipples. Light kisses filled open spots when my punishment was made clear.

The senses magnified the moment one loses control of any of the five. My sight was gone thanks to the blindfold. My hearing shot from a bad memory of having literally just met the crew a few hours prior to this moment. Touch was magnified. Taste was magnified. Both overly sexually stimulated. The scent of my sweetness filled the air, and I heard a moan from off in the distance. The thought of being watched aroused me more. The kissing stopped and the voice spoke again, "Be still."

Slowly I inhaled and exhaled through the first O. My punisher from below stood up and with a sense of laughter in his voice, he says, "Good girl."

Just as I began to smile and a second before I could start to wonder, my honey pot was resting along a different set of lips. A different like no other. Quick flitters of the tongue brought in the first O. The second one was stimulated by pure kisses. The joy he found came from him suckling on my clit and inner lips was evident as the second O came in hard and fast, but he didn't let up. I bit my bottom lip, still slowly inhaling between the Os but never breathing correctly during the moment.

Never more than three. I soon understood the severity of my crime. Talking shit on the internet had me in deep honey because it certainly wasn't shit. Pure Gold! The warm mouth of a third approached. My belief that I was going to be eaten to death was becoming more literal rather than figuratively. I found comfort in the way he slowed down. Tasting me as if my swollen clit simply needed healing from being previously devoured by the ravish beast before him. A mental note was made as the third, like the second did not reward me with compliments of being a good girl.

My squirms and wiggles increased with the fifth warm mouth. The urge to scream hadn't once approached while my movements put me in time out for five whole minutes. Just as I was approaching my ninth O, he stopped abruptly and sighs with disapproval. The familiar voice, disappointed as well says, "Don't move again."

Annoyed by the words being said aloud, I impatiently waited for the minutes to be up so that I could fully release my screams of pleasure in my highest octave. The crew anticipated the bratty behavior. It's what they wanted most of all. Just as the sixth settled into position and placed his warm mouth on me, I melted. His mouth wasn't warm at all. Cold actually. Extremely cold. Fresh and cold. Inhaling slowly was no more as I uncontrollably moaned, "Oo oo ooo oooo."

The light pinches on my nipples weren't so light anymore and the sweet kisses turned into full bites. I squirmed, wiggled, and swirled as much as my restraints allowed. My feet unbound as my sixth lifted my pelvis while he stood up. His thickness filled me up and finally my blindfold was lifted and there he was. Maybe it was just tunnel vision but all I seen was him. Maybe my imagination is running wild. A smile swept across my face as his hand wrapped around my throat while holding me up with the other and pumping in and out with ease. I begin to mumble the words slowly, "Are.....you...."

His tongue darted in and out of my mouth just for him to say, "You talk too much."

I smiled. Enjoying this meet and greet until the very end....

For ClickTight Rydaz

While working at IHOP in North Jackson, I met a cute little lady that expressed in great detail that she was GAY AF(as fuck)....as if I had a problem with her sexuality. I am first and foremost a shit talker and rather comfortable in my skin. Me talking shit is not determined by one's gender or sexuality. We're just matching each other's styles in some way or another. Understanding now that I am simply a product of my environment.....those grandma babies are just naturally carefree in everything we say and do.

Welp one day the grits were burnt and as I'm stirring the hella stiff grits I say, "Damn, Tay I thought you were going to be my bottom bitch but you can't make the grits!"

She looks at me with horror in her face and defends herself saying, "What?! I can make the grits!"

As if this is an actual conversation that should take place in a workplace but work with me.....so while I'm laughing she commences to prove her point and remakes the grits. They were indeed better and even had lots of butter in them. I knew I'd eventually write something inspired from that humors conversation.

Shrimp N' Grits

"Work that like how you should. Build me up, baby, give me that wood. Make it gangsta 'cause I like it real hood. Knock it down low, this how it go, oh-oh-oh" – Surprise by Chole Bailey

"Not too many times will there be compromise on my end." He leaned his shoulder against the door frame with a smirk and his arms folded. Another critique of the boudoir photoshoot. He's in a mood. I'm not playing along. I shouldn't respond but I do, saying, "Then maybe you should get behind the camera sir."

While licking his lips, he blushes. He's still entertaining this silliness, insisting to play the game saying, "I wouldn't have gotten the full calendar done. It's really a beautiful calendar."

I sigh as I attempt to walk away from the exchange being forced upon me when his arm goes up, blocking me from exiting. Hoping to speed up my exit, I say, "Thank you baby."

His arm didn't bulge. Wrong answer. I tilted my head to his slender frame just to see him lean forward, our lips inches apart as he demands, "Stop being so damn difficult and take your fucking clothes off."

I eyed him up and down and bit my lip helplessly failing at denying myself the guilty pleasures of a fine chocolate snack cake. Three years ago, I laughed when he approached for my phone number. *'He wouldn't last a week,'* I thought to myself. Now here I am soaking up my brand new Calvin Klein sweatsuit. It was self care day and I decided to chill out but here he is ready to put me to work on my only off day. He didn't force my sweatsuit off and yet I stood before him with nothing on waiting for him to say his next command. Muscle memory suggests that I rub my hands along the curves of my slim thick frame. He's nicer when I dance for him. He nods his head towards the armchair as a distraction. The moment I spin around in its direction is when his arms wrap around my waist. His chin snuggling into my shoulder blade for only a second and then quickly bends me over, ramming deep inside of me.

His thrusts were slow and hard. He showed no mercy as he intentionally tore down the walls of my lady pond. He wrapped my 30 inch middle part bust down around his hand at least twice and pulling out of me. I knew what my lover wanted because I wanted it too. I was on my knees taking in as much as I could. My only aim was to please my lover. His moans were the stamps of approval that I needed to hear the most. As I lifted his shaft, he dunked his balls in my mouth while massaging my breasts. My fingers swirled around in my lady pond until I was gagging on this greedy monster trying to rip through the back of my head.

After letting go of my hair, he placed his index finger underneath my chin lifting me to my feet. Dr. Jekyll and Mr. Hyde with this guy. This is why I didn't want to play the game. He kissed me and that was the last drop of sweetness that he had left about a funky ass boudoir shoot that he would have happily done had I asked. The way I had to listen to him taunting the photographer, the lighting, the edits, the idea itself. It took ten days for him to finally calm down and just fuck the shit out of me but he had to prove a point. He had to express himself. Make sure his feelings, thoughts, and concerns were heard and acknowledged by his other half. He made a scene every day for ten days. I walked around for ten fucking days waiting to get fucked and the man was whining about a boudoir photoshoot I did for him as a gift for his birthday.

Finally, he had my legs on his shoulders pounding away in my lady pond. This is all I wanted and this evil Mr. Know It All had me waiting ten whole damn days.....

10 DAYS AGO

I eyed the amount of butter he placed in his bowl of grits. High blood pressure and clogged arteries, he'd have for sure as I spoke softly, "Baby, that's too much butter."

He paused and with a scoff commenced to adding at least three more unhealthy heapings of butter and said, "I wasn't even going to say anything about how you burned the grits."

I sighed reflecting on the fact that I wasn't Susie Homemaker nor was I trying to be. I couldn't boil water but here I was trying to fix the man something before our trip to New York. Ungrateful is what he was! Instead of sitting beside my headache and pretending to enjoy breakfast, I went ahead and cleaned the kitchen. My attempt at avoiding any more critique from the man before we headed to the airport.

His footsteps were heavy as he walked up behind me planting light kisses along my shoulder blades. He was in a mood ready to play this God awful game of his as he started, "How you from the Delta and can't cook grits?!"

With an ass smack to further prove his point, I replied, "I might look the part but I don't even eat grits baby and you know this."

In a singsong voice, he says, "Good because I loooooovvvvvveeeeee grits!"

He held me close, reaching underneath my short flowy moo moo, slowly inserting his fingers inside of me. Sliding from behind me in order to face me, I leaned back against the counter watching him slowly descend unto his knees to reiterate exactly how much he loved *'Girls Raised In The South'*

For Travian Rainey (My Pig Faced Broski)

From the very beginning of truly diving into this writing career and author life, I knew that I would do a collection of short erotic stories and yet I had no idea how. Story after story seemed boring. I definitely wanted something with a little more pizzazz in the set up at least. Hence this cutesy little collection set up in a way where each story is in itself a dedication to the actual inspiration behind the story as well as a little note to my readers.

Hoping to truly share how anything and anyone can become the inspiration and motivation to many pieces of art...remixing a simple story shared over many bonfires and cold Coronas....

ShowKaze

"Wats happen wats tha bizness.... I can't believe I did this... A whole month no sex... I keep it real low plex... All I'm sayin wats next don't take it out of context.... Play doctor (let me check)... Wanna play construction (let me wreck)" – Blow Your Back Out by Tha Joker

He dashed into the library from wrestling practice almost forty minutes late to the tutoring lesson he was having with Harper. Things were starting off on a bad note as Harper already had an underlying hatred for jocks with Delvin Walls being at the top of her list. He was well known around campus as a party guy and a ladies' man which she wanted no parts of it. Going against her better judgment, she agreed to this simple biology lesson since she needed the money to finish her art project, unlike Delvin who was in desperate need to ace his exam now that finals had approached them. Harper shook her head looking at her watch remembering how Delvin pleaded with her about his grades and needing to keep his scholarship. He hurried to the table panting, trying to whisper his apologies. The librarian shushing him as he did not try hard enough for her liken. Annoyed, Harper motioned for him to sit down, and they dug into the lesson.

It took an hour before Harper actually loosened up to Delvin. She was giving him a hard time on purpose until Delvin flipped the script on her. Even though she despised being corrected by somebody like him, Harper was beginning to see that Delvin was not just a simple-minded jock but that it was some brains under that helmet as well. A smile crept across her face as she began to hate him a little less. She spoke coyly, "And to think I thought you were just a dumb jock."

His voice was smooth as he bragged, "Of course I know a little thing or two." He had a certain charm about him along with his smarts was making quite the impression on Harper. It helped that he was easy on the eyes as well. She could tell from just looking at him that he did not hear the words, no, too often and although she would never admit it aloud, she was yearning for a different kind of biology lesson. Delvin continued, "Especially things dealing with the human body." His eyes scanned her body in the most obvious of ways causing Harper to blush. It was clear that Delvin was on the same page. Her 5'9 slim figure caught his eye weeks ago when he noticed her walking to class carrying nothing but her books with a calculator wearing these big nerdy looking glasses. She pulled the look off in the sexiest way. It made Delvin want to get to know her and lucky for him, he had the perfect reason with his exam. He wondered where Harper's mind truly was as he decided to test the waters by asking, "Did you know that certain pressure points on your body can send relaxing and stimulating tingles all over your body when they are touched just right?"

Her eyebrow rose signaling to Delvin that he had piqued her interest. She tried not to look so defeated by his mesmerizing demeanor as she replied, "Oh really?"

Delvin knew she had fallen as he had seen it happen so many times before. He licked his lips, "Yes really." His charm went on, "Since we are in the library, I'd like to show you the books dealing with what I'm talking about. They're on the third floor."

To his surprise, she agreed and started gathering her things. He had hoped she would but did not think she would really go for it. Harper had heard of the stories about the third floor. It was not exclusive but not everybody can say they have experienced it. It contained a bunch of old dusty books inside a couple of forgotten classrooms. It is pretty much a library version of lovers' lane which means anything can happen. There are spots like these all over campus. Harper has heard a few things about them since she has been here a little longer than Delvin, but she has yet to explore any of them. The opportunity never knocked until now. She knew exactly where he was trying to take this.

As they stepped off the elevator, Delvin guided her into an unlocked study room. On the wall near the dry-erase board hung a karma sutra poster. Delvin nervously chuckled at the cornball that placed it there, but it was the very thing that caught Harper's attention. She stared intensely at the poster until she spun around demanding, "So show me these points you were talking about Mr. Delvin Walls."

Swiftly he walked to the karma sutra chart and pointed, "Now if I kiss you on this spot that's above your neck and behind your ear, it'll send this stimulating sensation down your spine."

"Is that so?" boasted Harper.

"No doubt." He responded, "Allow me to demonstrate." He stepped closer to her asking, "May I?"

She spoke softly, "Proceed."

He gently pulled back her hair placing sweet tender kisses on her neck leading up behind her ear. He could feel her body shudder with every kiss she received. With a faint voice, she mumbled, "What are the other points?"

He explained between kisses, "If I move along your collarbone, these kisses will make your temperature rise."

She whispered, "Show me."

Eagerly he complied and gave her what she asked for. Without hesitation, he carefully removed her shirt and passionately planted kisses along her collarbone while he unsnapped the hooks to her bra. Delvin caressed her breasts as she moaned, "More." His tongue rotated around her perfect gumdrop nipples, making her crave him more.

He posed as he lightly nibbled her nipples, "Can I show you what would make your knees weak?"

Between staggered breaths, she uttered, "Yes!"

Within no time her knees started to buckle as he rolled his tongue down to her belly button from her breasts. He laid her down on an old teacher's desk. She bit down on her bottom lip when she felt his kisses on her inner thighs. Her moans grew louder as he pushed her panties to the side and slid two fingers into her moist juicy prize. He soothed her aches as he prepared to demonstrate one of the most important pressure points of all. One she would soon become addicted to. Delvin eased down and begin to roll his tongue around the tip of her pearl still fondling her prize. Harper felt a surge of pure fire course through her body. Deliberately, he gripped her thigh with his free hand and took his sweet time devouring her. She dared to pull away, but little did she know, things were just getting started.

Delvin stood up with a smile on his face after he had wiped her juices off. He could tell from the look in her eyes that she had another pressure point she wanted to be touched by him. He slid her panties off and placed them in his pockets with a smirk on his face. Her eyes widen with excitement seeing the elephant trunk that he gripped in his hand. He entered her with ease making Harper roll her hips in pleasure while Delvin deeply pumped in and out. Her nails dug into his back pulling him deeper inside. He lifted her legs and placed them on his shoulders, not knowing this was her favorite position. His strokes went from deep and gentle to hard and rough, but she loved every second of it. Seeing Harper handling his strokes like a pro, Delvin picked her up from the desk while she wrapped her legs around his waist. He placed her against the karma sutra poster without missing a beat in his rhythm. He continued to hammer Harper until sweat poured from both of their bodies as paint chips fell to the floor from the loud scratches that Harper was making on the wall.

They climaxed within seconds of each other. Delvin stood with one hand on the wall holding him up as Harper slowly unwrapped her legs from around his waist. As they got dressed Delvin enticed, "I look forward to our next study session."

Barely any breath to speak Harper joked, "As do I, Mr. Delvin Walls."

When they were ready to part ways, she looked at Delvin with a smile as he whispered in her ear, "Call me whenever you're free."

If only he had known the monster, he created that night......

For Delvin Walls (ShowKaze)

Be sure to also check out KC's first novel, a romantic suspense titled, *Melanin Midas Empire,* also available in paperback and ebook.

Excerpt from

Melanin Midas Empire
A Southern Salute

Tylertown, Mississippi
1915 AD
-The Hidden King-

He walked in with sweat dripping on the rustic wooden floors that creaked an inch louder with each step that he took, in search of my hidden king. The bounty hunter was armed with a shotgun and orders from German soldiers of Brune to kill my child on sight. They believed that he was an abomination and would one day fulfill a prophecy, causing the world to end. There was talk of ancient scrolls and how one day, he would come in the last hour. Those scrolls went on to warn the people of the many impure spirits that were already roaming about the land. Word of the German soldiers had traveled fast to the nearby town of McComb, Mississippi and warned the village that was entrusted in guarding our future king that our God had appointed.

Quickly, I gathered him up in my arms as the bounty hunter drew closer, placing him in a small wooden box asleep and sliding it under our bed. I fell to my knees as the door swung open. There stood the bounty hunter, the sheriff, and the constable ready to take my child. Tears rolled down my cheeks as I prayed to my God in a language unknown to my trespassers. The sheriff yelled out, "WITCH!" and yet I continued to pray while listening to the cold calculated sounds of the bounty hunter's steel toe boots looking to devour my innocent black king. The constable snatched me up by my arms and screamed in my face, "Where's the Brunner boy?!"

Vigorously, I shook my head with fear consuming me, refusing to give them the answers they desperately wanted. He slapped me back down to the hard wooden floor with the back side of my face, causing blood to flow out freely in the mixture of my tears. I sobbed harder to my God as the bounty hunter, the sheriff, and the constable trashed this little shack of a house looking for anything that would lead them to my hidden king. When they believed that my child was elsewhere, they left, leaving the door wide open. I continued to sob on the floor, thankful that my sweet baby boy wasn't found.

After cleaning myself up as well as the shack, I fed and changed my little king. I slowly rocked him in my arms, as I hummed heavenly hymns to him. Life had been hell from the moment I took my first breath. I had prayed for better and yet better wasn't a word I even knew the definition of but looking into the beautiful brown eyes of my child, brought a warmth to me that transcended beyond space and time. Constantly, I wondered how I would protect him in this cruel world when I, myself, was on the run hiding out in this foreign country so far away from my home in Kingston, Jamaica. My only hope in this life was to see my son age up well despite him being the product of a secret love affair with a German Lord and if found alive, we'd both be killed.

Jackson, Mississippi
2005 AD
– 90 YEARS LATER –

Chanice

IN THE MIDDLE OF SEPTEMBER, Linda had managed to get all seven of her living and jail free siblings together for a birthday celebration in honor of their mother, Myrtis Lee Rogers. She was turning seventy-eight years old and was the mother of eleven children, five girls and six boys. Having already lost two of her sons to death and one incarcerated for life, this celebration was one of many that we all hoped to cherish. Most of her children had gone on to get married and live their own lives except the two playboys in the family, Jonas and the baby of them all Keith. Didn't seem like they would ever find a sweet lady to settle down with. Two of her girls had left Mississippi in hopes of a better life with Margaret living in Nashville and Beverly living in Indianapolis. Myrtis wasn't at all an easy woman to impress as she sat with a frown watching her second oldest daughter parade around bragging about this salute that she cared nothing about.

Linda listed off the weekend's menu as she said, "Since it's Friday, we're having fried fish. You know Mama, I think fish just don't taste the same any other day. Fried fish was just made for Fridays. Now on Saturday, I might do some spaghetti and Sunday I'll do some collard greens with hamhocks, candied yams, mac and cheese, some cornbread, and some fried chicken. I already got your coconut cake and rainbow cake made and sitting on the cake stands on the table there. I know Beverly gone want me to help her preach and pray over the family. Oh yeah Mama this gone be the best salute ever!"

It's been said that if you want to make God laugh then tell him your plans so maybe Linda felt the need to try her hand at being a comedian because as soon as I got home from school, my great grandma Myrtis had already upset my grandma Linda and her fidgeting the entire time. I called my grandma Meme and my great grandma, Grandma. It was weird to others but it always made sense to me as I was the first great grandchild of Myrtis and yet adopted to my legally blind grandma Linda. Being legally blind didn't mean she couldn't see. It only meant that she couldn't see as well as the rest of us. I learned over time that she seen what she wanted to see and one thing she loved to do was brag even if that meant over exaggerating the truth. Meme claims I was only two or three years old when she was leaving out of the room and I couldn't stand the thought of her leaving me, so I ran behind her screaming, "Me me me me me me me me!" I don't recall ever asking about the nickname especially since my entire family loved to put emphasis on the fact that she was MY Meme. Never bothered me because she was MY Meme.

We had just moved to Jackson a few years ago, leaving the small town of Quitman, Mississippi in our rearview forever. I was young and didn't understand the fights a mother and daughter sometimes had but what I knew was that Meme was tired of taking care of her mother and she wanted to live her own life. For eleven years, I never seen Meme ever entertain a man and within six months of moving to Jackson, Meme had married Luther. As long as she was happy, then I was happy. She told me all about how they had known each other for years from working together at Mississippi Industries for the Blind and that they were always respectful of each other. Of all the daughters Myrtis had, it was my Meme that she had this overprotective nature with, and she wasn't at all happy with her marrying that man and showed contempt whenever she could. Meme simply ignored it and loved on her mother anyway.

This left Keith as Myrtis' caretaker for as much as she'd allow. She preferred for her baby girl Eunice to come from Jackson, Mississippi and see to her but she was too busy being a city girl with her husband to go back to being a country bumpkin in Clarke County. Keith didn't mind it too much. Being married and having his own little family was something he believed would come along eventually and he wasn't rushing anything with anybody so taking care of his old, crippled mother wasn't too bad until he was ready to get out and find trouble like any playboy. Naturally, her loneliness caused her to lash out at people sometimes. Meme would tell me to look over her mother as she was just old and senile.

Whenever they came to visit, Myrtis would sit in the recliner beside the front door that faced the hallway. A lot of times, I'd think she was sleeping and so I'd never speak on my way out the door hoping not to disturb her rest but whenever I got home from school, I'd be in trouble for not speaking to my grandma before heading off to school. I'd constantly have to apologize for what I always thought was the right thing to do. This day was different. I spoke regardless. I was tired of being in trouble for trying to be nice. Sure enough, she was sleep but I still spoke and I went on to my room. The second my room door closed, she was praying for understanding, believing that I was a troubled fourteen year old in need of help.

Instantly, she felt the emotions of a similar past pain that she once felt when she was only twelve years old. Her parents had died leaving her to raise all five of her siblings alone in 1939 in Tylertown, Mississippi. Four years later and she was giving birth to her first child, Ethel. Myrtis was a beautiful woman of light complexion with ginger colored hair while Cherokee and white ran through her veins. There wasn't a girl from her line that didn't understand what she learned fast and that was that beauty was a blessing and a curse. She shared with Meme what she believed to be true as she spoke softly, "Lin, I need to tell you something about Niecy."

Whenever there was gossip, Meme was first in line but whenever there were words about me, she was quick to dismiss it. As far as Meme was concerned, I could do no wrong and even if I did do wrong, it wasn't as bad as what others had done. She knew that Myrtis had a temper on her, and she also knew that Myrtis was hardly ever wrong about the things she felt after she prayed for understanding. Myrtis and Linda were thick as thieves and stayed discussing the inner workings of the Brunner family. I'm sure Meme had this famous perplexed look on her face as she sat up straight and listened to what her mother had to say but ready to dismiss any and everything that wasn't for the good of her Niecy. Meme sighed and replied, "What is it mama?"

Myrtis looked down the hallway of the house and around to make sure no one heard what she was about to say before speaking low, "You need to talk to Niecy. She just came in and went straight to her room as if she's in trouble for something."

Meme quickly waved her hands in disregard to what her mother was saying as she replied, "Oh mama you know how teenagers can be. She's just on that computer or on the phone with her friends is all. She's not in trouble. The girl don't do nothing."

Myrtis shook her head understanding that Meme wouldn't be able to see this kind of pain if she's never felt it herself. She had protected her from as many dangers in the world as she could and even at seventy-eight years old, Myrtis still didn't mind protecting her, but she needed her daughter to understand so she spoke freely and said, "Lin, that child done been raped. You need to talk to her."

With a feeling of failure rushing over, Meme refused to hear this bullshit coming from her mother's mouth, but she knew better than to disrespect her in any way, shape, or form. Myrtis stayed with a pistol in her purse, loaded, and ready at all times. It was a hard pill to swallow for any mother, but she stood up and with full confidence and lied to her mother's face as she said, "Don't worry. I'll talk to her but let me get back to frying this fish. I think Margaret and Beverly will be pulling in soon and I want everything done in time."

Myrtis wasn't a stranger to a lie. She herself had told a few and yet she looked at her daughter with disgust ready to take her crooked up right hand and bop her ditzy ass right in the head with her copper colored cane. She wanted to go express her love for me and understanding because she knew she wasn't wrong, but she knew Meme would make a scene. It took some time but during the visits she made after the salute, Myrtis expressed to me all of her love in the best way that she could. She certainly wasn't wrong. I had been raped and for years I blamed myself trying to understand what I did to make this strange man look at me and take my innocence. At thirteen, I wasn't at all trying to dress like I was going to freaknik. I wasn't all in his face being grown. No matter how many times I replayed the scene in my head wondering what I could've done differently to prevent this, I found myself left with more questions than answers and the only conclusion I had was that it was my fault.

Maybe if I hadn't gone outside to play. Maybe I should've stopped hanging out with that seventeen year old girl like my Meme told me.

Maybe I should've walked away sooner when I felt uncomfortable watching him and that girl talk and joke around. Those were the only maybes I had to stop him because within seconds he had turned around from that girl and ran up to me, lifting me in the air and over his shoulder. I kicked and punched his back, and it was as if he skipped happily into his house. Into his bedroom, where he placed me on the floor. Still fighting. I fought as hard as I could to not even weigh a hundred pounds. My efforts to get him off of me were futile. I watched a smile creep across his face as he pushed my legs to my head and tugged my jeans off my bottom. I was balled up like a fucking pretzel unable to do anything but take it.

When he was done, he got up laughing as I pulled my jeans up and stormed out of his house directly into his gold car. He had wires hanging down and all I wanted was to hurt him like he had hurt me, and I had no idea how to hurt him, so I just pulled the wires until they broke. Tweet and her little cousin laughed as she said, "Dang what took y'all so long? Were y'all having sex?"

I hated myself. I hated being outside. The one place I used to love so much in Quitman. A true country girl at heart. Loving the animals. The grass. The trees. The cool breeze. Hearing the birds chirp and watching the flowers bloom. I was the weird one dancing in the rain on May 1st believing that it would bring me good fortune. I found peace being outside and now all I wanted to do was disappear and be forgotten. I wanted to run away. I wanted to never exist. Secluding myself in my room was my only option and I happily took it every day while allowing the actions of a grown ass man to cause me to cast blame on myself.

This salute was already starting off on a bad foot, something Myrtis knew all about as well as she massaged the old incision scar on her left knee while humming, "Mmmmmmhmmmm"

Despite the sour undertones, it was a beautiful sight seeing the Brunner family together. They may have had their differences, but you wouldn't have known as Keith was the ringleader of all trouble related activities. Enticing his older siblings to take a step on the bad side. Beverly had become a pastor, but she didn't mind a game of spades and a little wine on the side with her baby brother. As long as there was a case of Coca-Colas and a bottle of Jack, then Ethel and Eunice would be in attendance. Sweet Margaret and Meme's twin brother Joe just followed suit along with everybody else. There wasn't a show without the Mississippi Pimp himself, Jonas. His high yella self, sporting his Sunday's best on a Tuesday, donning his pimpalicious cane with a red feather in his hat always made him the man of the hour.

    The children of the older siblings were now grown enough to partake in the Brunner family shenanigans that they used to only hear about. Katrina and JohnJohn were the only ones to stop by and that's only because Katrina promised me that she would so that I could see my baby brother. My mom didn't get along with Meme and she certainly didn't care to get on Myrtis' bad side either, so she felt it was best to stay away. She wasn't everybody's cup of tea after shacking up with JohnJohn's father for the past fourteen years which was proving to had been about the worse decision that she could've made but what was she to do? Blame it on drugs? Blame it on love? Blame it on lust? None of it mattered. She was in it for the long haul no matter how miserable she was on the inside. She was able to get away and spend time with her family without her warden breathing down her neck or causing a bunch of chaos. He was too busy at home in Battlefield with a crack pipe in one hand and a lighter in the other.

    Herr and Keith shared a doobie on the front porch and laughed about their teen years as they were only four years apart in age but so much had changed now that they were both parents. He took a hit and spoke freely, "Katrina, Niecy is an amazing kid. You should spend more time with her. Get to know her better. She's your only daughter. She made you a mother."

    As nonchalant as always, my mother shrugged as she sighed and said, "I want to but her Meme ain't gone let me and Niecy ain't nothing how

I used to be. You know I was wild Uncle Keith! I stayed out shaking my ass somewhere getting into some of everything. Niecy is a good girl. She doesn't listen to the music that I listen to. She doesn't like any of the stuff that I like. She may look like me but that's more Linda's daughter than she is mine."

Surely remembering my mother's wild days, Keith shook his head, exhaled, and replied, "Nah Katrina, she's more like you than you know. She just hides it better than you ever did. You got to really get her to open up to you and you'll see. I wish I could have a daughter as amazing as her."

My mother was a lot like Myrtis, always picking up on the not so obvious as she coughed and then replied, "What about baby girl? You don't think she's yours huh?"

Keith sighed as he said, "I know she's not, but I don't mind being a father to a fatherless child. Especially a little girl. They need to be protected at all costs." In that moment, I was walking up the stairs with a crisp ten dollar bill in my hands coming to hug my mom. Uncle Keith smiled and said, "Think fast" while attempting to rip the money out of my hand only for me to grip it harder, preparing for was over this ten dollar bill. I don't know what that man was thinking trying to take my little coins like that! All he did was laugh hard as ever as he said, "Smart kid."

It wasn't long before Keith left on a trouble run with the Mississippi Pimp and Meme's twin brother Joe. My cousins, Sheena, Janay, and Regine decided to go outside and play. Of course, I tagged along but as in any black neighborhood there was fresh meat on the playground and all the boys came out like sharks to chum. I wanted no parts of the fuckery because aside from the rumor mill saying I had given it up freely, Keith and Myrtis were in town and what Myrtis couldn't do, Keith would so I went back to the steps and sat down on the porch. My cousins could do whatever they wanted to do. Sheena, however, followed closely behind because she too knew that Keith and Myrtis wasn't hearing shit about why we were talking to any boy. For poor Regine, she had to make a decision and make it fast because Sheena and I were already back across the street, and it was literally every man for themselves. Regine was the youngest at only ten years old and she didn't want to leave her sister alone with those boys, but her sister was the oldest of them all. Janay was sixteen years old with her foot propped up on the fence of the basketball court and about ten boys surrounding her. She had a smile plastered across her face, enjoying every second of the attention these sharks were giving her while Sheena and I watched from a distance as Regine yelled out, "Come on Janay!" before running across the street and leaving her sister to fend for herself.

All hell broke loose when Keith pulled back up from dropping off his brothers. He stormed into the house after running the boys off, demanding to beat every one of us because we all knew better than to be outside around those boys in the first fucking place. Everybody knew how angry Keith could get. Everybody knew that Keith was the protector of every girl in the Brunner family. From his mother down to his baby niece. If there was ever a problem, they knew to call Keith as they had done so many many times before. Eunice tried to calm him down as she said, "Well what done happened Keith? What did they do?"

He yelled, "All of them out there fucking off with those boys. It was about twenty of them trying to get them down! How the hell y'all in this fucking house and they outside fucking with these boys and y'all don't know shit?"

Eunice shook her head and said, "Oh I know not mine!" She yelled out, "Sheena!" Her light sugar biscuit colored daughter walked in, and she asked, "Were you out there fooling around with some boys and don't you lie?!"

Sheena shook her head and said, "No ma'am. That was Janay."

Fear fell on Margaret's face as she knew her niece wasn't lying. Janay was hot in the ass and the whole damn family knew it, but she couldn't stand to see her child get beat for it. Beverly noticed the strained look on her big sister's face, and she stood up to protest in righteousness as she spoke, "Now Keith, you need to calm down because these are teenage girls with hormones. They weren't doing nothing but talking."

Keith yelled out, "BULLSHIT!!! They were seconds away from fucking these girls outside and you want to preach about some fucking hormones. Ain't that how you ended up with LeShonda at sixteen?!"

The atmosphere had changed beyond repair, but Meme still had to try and calm down the situation as it was her house. She spoke softly, "But Keith it wasn't all the girls. It was just Janay and she do need her ass beat."

Keith shook his head and replied, "No, Lin! They all need their ass beat. They were all outside and they all knew better. Niecy, Sheena, and Regine just sat there and watched. Anything could've happened to Janay and y'all in this house not knowing a damn thing!"

Meme wasn't about to let anybody put their hands on me in our house, so she stood her ground and said, "I don't care who you beat but you ain't beating mine!"

He looked around as if he was Denzel Washington in *'Training Day'*, seeing all five sisters stand against him along with his mother sitting silently unable to utter a word in his defense. She too felt like he had taken it a little too far. Keith nodded his head in understanding as he said, "Don't call me when they all get pregnant and raped because you were too busy screaming *'Not Mine'* because I damn sholl ain't gone answer."

Instantly, Beverly remembered how she called Keith with tears in her eyes only some years ago. It was before she had moved out of Mississippi and most likely the very reason that she did. In the middle of the night, Keith had become irate and told Meme to get the gun and put some clothes on. I remember everything so vividly as we all loaded into Myrtis' grey Cadillac. As I sat in the middle, Keith rushed to the back door and swung it open. He spoke soft but firm as he said, "Don't touch it Niecy."

He slid the double barrel shotgun across my lap, and I surely did not fucking touch it. We traveled from Quitman to Jackson at full speed to

Beverly's house by Provine. Her second husband had her curled up in fetal position on the kitchen floor kicking her ribs in. That night, her baby brother saved her life, and it wasn't a moment in which he wouldn't do it all over again. She had a finalized divorce and a new outlook on life before packing up her life and moving to Indiana but in this particular moment, her past was her past. She was a pastor now and she was hurt to see her baby brother so eager to whoop on these babies as she said, "You need to calm down and see things from our point of view."

Keith looked her dead in her eyes and spoke boldly saying, "And you damn sholl bet not ever call me again."

With a belief that she would never need to ever again, her eyes filled up with tears as shook her head. She pointed her index finger right in his face and boldly said, "You're dead to me Keith."

The salute was over. Beverly left out that same night heading back to Indianapolis while Margaret headed out the next day for Nashville. A riff had torn my family into shreds because of harsh words and unspoken hurts. In the car heading back to Quitman, Mississippi, Myrtis said to Keith, "Death is about to hit this family and it's coming in a set of three. I pray you find a woman to love you. I pray I get to see you, my baby boy, happily married before I leave this Earth."

Fear engulfed Keith as he knew some things just shouldn't be said.

Acknowledgements

To every reader that has enjoyed this collection of short stories.....
THANK YOU SO MUCH!!!
Peace, Love, & Blessings
KC

Also by Katrina Chanice

KC's Emporium of Wet Dreams
Melanin Midas Empire